?? ASK A ?? DINOSAUR

Olivia Brookes

PowerKiDS
press.

New York

Published in 2009 by The Rosen Publishing Group, Inc.
29 East 21st Street, New York, NY 10010

Created and produced by: Julia Bruce,
Rachel Coombs, Nicholas Harris, Sarah Hartley, and
Erica Simms, Orpheus Books Ltd

U.S. editor: Kara Murray

Illustrated by: Peter David Scott (The Art Agency)
Other illustrations by: Nicki Palin and
Alessandro Rabatti

Consultant: Chris Jarvis
The Oxford University Museum
of Natural History, England

Library of Congress Cataloging-in-Publication Data

Brookes, Olivia.
A dinosaur / Olivia Brookes.
p. cm. — (Ask)
Includes index.
ISBN 978-1-4358-2513-0 (library binding)
1. Dinosaurs—Juvenile literature. I. Title.
QE861.5.B756 2009
567.9—dc22
2008005815

Manufactured in China

contents

Introduction

Come on a journey with us to meet some of the oldest life on Earth. Follow the story of how the dinosaurs came to rule Earth for 160 million years—long before there were any people. Listen to a *Tyrannosaurus rex* as he tells you how he hunts down his prey. Find out which dinosaurs had feathers and what it was like to be a baby dinosaur. We can show you why these great reptiles died out and what happened after they were gone. You will meet a bird large enough to eat a horse and watch early humans like you hunt woolly mammoths. But first, take a dive with us into the warm waters of the Cambrian ocean and see how it all began.

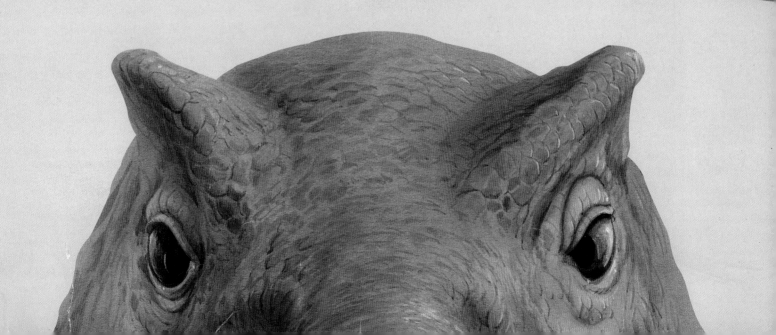

What Were the First Living Things?

I am anomalocaris, the largest predator here in the warm seas of the Cambrian period. I'm as long as your arm. I eat almost anything. I grab my prey with my arms and push it into my spine-rimmed mouth.

Jellyfish look just the same as in your time.

The hard spines on wiwaxia's back make it hard to eat.

Some creatures try to defend themselves against me and other predators. Hallucigenia's long, sharp spines are pretty scary. I think I'll try for easier prey, like those soft, juicy aysheaias feeding on the pink sponges.

Opabinia has five eyes and a long trunk, like an elephant's.

I am a trilobite. I have a hard shell and many legs. My large eyes are made up of lots of lenses, so I can see all around me. If I see danger coming, I quickly dig a hole and hide in the soft sand of the ocean floor.

When Did Reptiles First Appear?

After living in the water for years, we lobe-finned fish have begun looking for food on land. With our strong, fleshy fins, we crawl ashore to eat.

There is plenty of life on land now. It's the Carboniferous period. The world is warm and wet. Plants have been growing on land for millions of years. There are huge trees and ferns everywhere. I am eryops, an amphibian. I live part of my life in the water and part of it on land, but I can't move very fast on land. I can breathe air, but I have to lay my eggs in the water. I eat fish and I also catch bugs.

There are lots of giant bugs to eat in these forests. This dragonfly has wings that are 2 feet (.6 m) across! Some of the centipedes are more than 3 feet (.9 m) long and as thick as your arm.

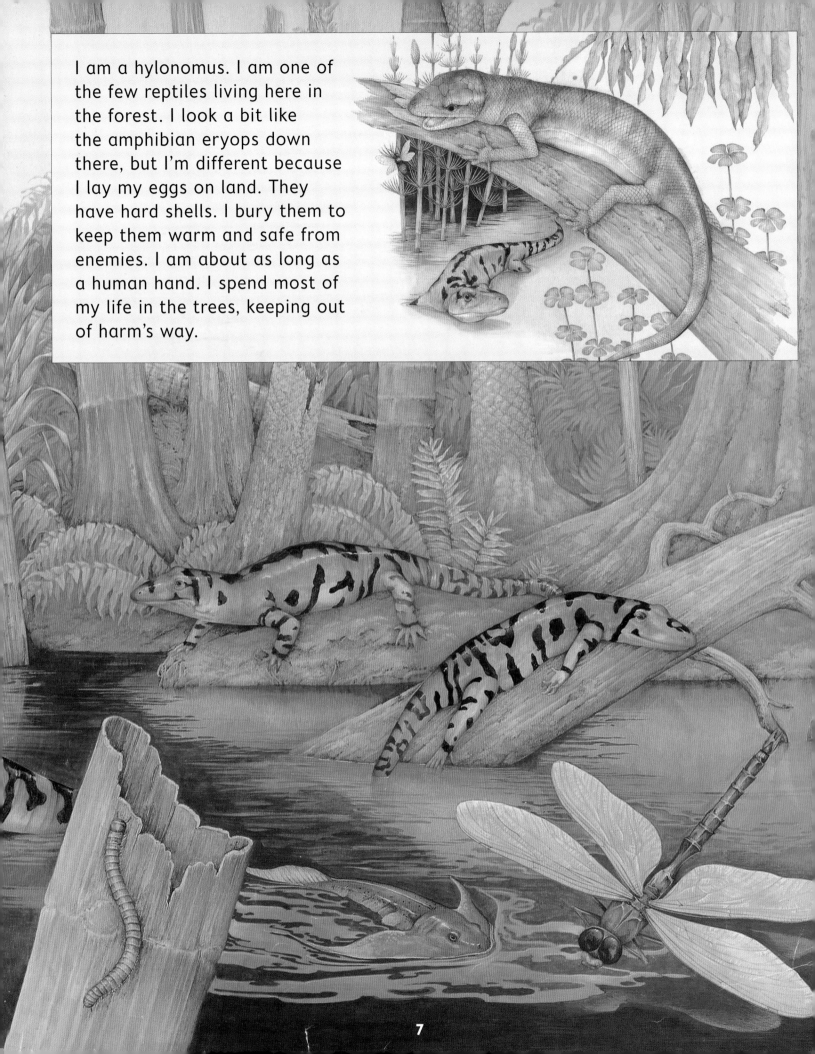

I am a hylonomus. I am one of the few reptiles living here in the forest. I look a bit like the amphibian eryops down there, but I'm different because I lay my eggs on land. They have hard shells. I bury them to keep them warm and safe from enemies. I am about as long as a human hand. I spend most of my life in the trees, keeping out of harm's way.

How Did Plant-Eating Dinosaurs Live?

I am a mamenchisaurus, a plant-eating dinosaur. It is the Jurassic period and I live in what is now China. With my long neck, I can reach high into the branches for the best leaves. My big, flat teeth are good for chewing leaves. I have to eat many, many leaves to stay alive. So many, in fact, that I also have to swallow stones to help my body grind the leaves up and digest them.

These little pterosaurs are helping me by picking bugs off my skin.

8

My babies like to eat soft fern leaves. These babies will grow up to have the longest necks of any dinosaur in the world. They will be at least 50 feet (15 m) long.

Our large herd has to keep moving to find more food. Moving around is dangerous for young, very old, and weak members of our herd. Predators can easily attack them. They also get hungry and tired.

What Was It Like to Be a Baby Dinosaur?

I am a duck-billed dinosaur called maiasaura. My name means "good mother lizard." Before she laid her eggs, my mother found a safe place for a nest close to many other nests. We now live together in a large herd. Here, I am just a few months old.

2 My mom laid 25 eggs. They are each the size of a melon and have hard shells. My brothers and sisters and I grew inside them. This is me, almost ready to hatch.

1 My mother made her nest from mud. Then she covered our eggs with leaves and dead plants to keep them warm.

3 Even with my mother standing guard, sneaky, egg-eating dinosaurs sometimes try to steal eggs from the nest. I was a lucky one!

4 This is us coming out of our eggs. We broke the tops off our eggs and wiggled free. We could walk around as soon as we came out. Boy, was I hungry!

5 Luckily, our mother had some juicy ferns ready. We duck-billed dinosaurs eat only plants. We'll probably grow 10 times bigger than we are now.

6 I am now old enough to join the herd and find food by myself. The herd will travel across the country until we find a good place to eat plants.

Why Did Some Dinosaurs Hunt in Packs?

We are deinonychus, which means "terrible claw." We are only about your height, but we can easily attack and kill prey much larger than we are. That's because we've learned how to hunt together.

When we spot our prey, like this tenontosaurus, we hide in the bushes around it. Then we jump out and attack!

Today's victim is old and alone, separated from its herd. We are all around it. I race in first and leap onto its back, digging in my claws. The others are right behind me, closing in from all sides.

This is our secret weapon, a very sharp, curved claw on each of our back feet. It is so large that we have to hold it up out of the way while we are walking or running. When we attack our prey, we push it forward into the prey. The claw can tear flesh easily and kill with one blow.

Even an old tenontosaurus like this one could defend itself against just one of us. It could strike out with its tail or stamp with its feet. But together we can bring down this large, slow plant eater in a very short time. We can feast for days on such a large, fleshy dinosaur.

Our strong back legs and long, stiff tails help us to balance as we twist and turn while running.

How Did Dinosaurs Defend Themselves?

With so many predators, like allosaurus, around, we plant eaters need to defend ourselves. I am stegosaurus. I live in the Late Jurassic period in North America. I'm very slow, but my spiny tail is a good weapon and my skin is strong.

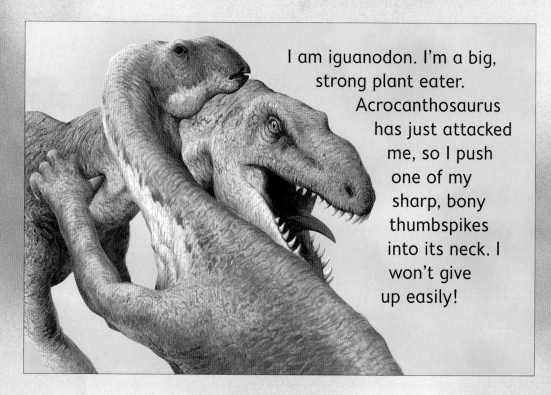

I am iguanodon. I'm a big, strong plant eater. Acrocanthosaurus has just attacked me, so I push one of my sharp, bony thumbspikes into its neck. I won't give up easily!

The plates on my back are not actually armor. When I'm cold, I stand in the sun. Blood inside the plates warms up and then goes through my body.

I am a talarurus. I have bony armor all over my body. I also have a heavy clubbed tail to strike out at predators.

I am styracosaurus. I have a sharp horn on my nose. Spines around my head keep the back of my neck safe.

A little ornitholestes like me has only one choice: run away!

Did Some Dinosaurs Have Feathers?

I am one of the strangest dinosaurs you'll ever meet. My name is therizinosaurus, and I live in China. I am covered in feathers, but I can't fly. I have a small head and a large bill. I also have huge claws on my front wings. I eat plants, using my claws to pull down branches and eat the leaves.

I am one of the very first birds. My name is archaeopteryx. Like a dinosaur, I have sharp teeth, claws on my wings, and a bony tail. But I also have feathers and can fly.

We caudopteryxes have feathered tails. We look like birds, but we're really dinosaurs.

Like archaeopteryx, I, confuciusornis, am a bird, too. Males like me show off our tail feathers to impress females. I use my wing claws to move around in the trees.

I'm a velociraptor from China. Like a bird, I'm actually warm blooded. My feathers keep me warm. I cannot fly, but I'm a fast runner. I have very sharp teeth. I also use the curved claws on my back feet to kill my prey. But this protoceratops here is heavier and stronger than I am!

How Did Some Reptiles Fly?

I am pteranodon. I live in Late Cretaceous North America. I live at the same time as the giants *Tyrannosaurus rex* and triceratops. I am neither a dinosaur nor a bird. I am actually a pterosaur, or flying reptile. I eat by flying low over the sea and picking fish up in my jaws. Unlike other pterosaurs, I don't have any teeth, so I swallow the fish or save them for later in a pouch under my bill.

We eudimorphodons are pterosaurs living in the Jurassic period. We eat fish, too, but with our sharp teeth.

I am a rhamphorhyncus. My teeth are long and pointy and stick out from my jaws. They are just the right shape for catching fish. I catch fish easily from just below the water's surface. I also have a throat pouch to store fish in if I don't want to eat now or to save them for my babies.

I spend most of my time flying in the air with my wings stretched out. I can stay in the air for hours. It's much easier for me to fly than to walk because my legs are very weak.

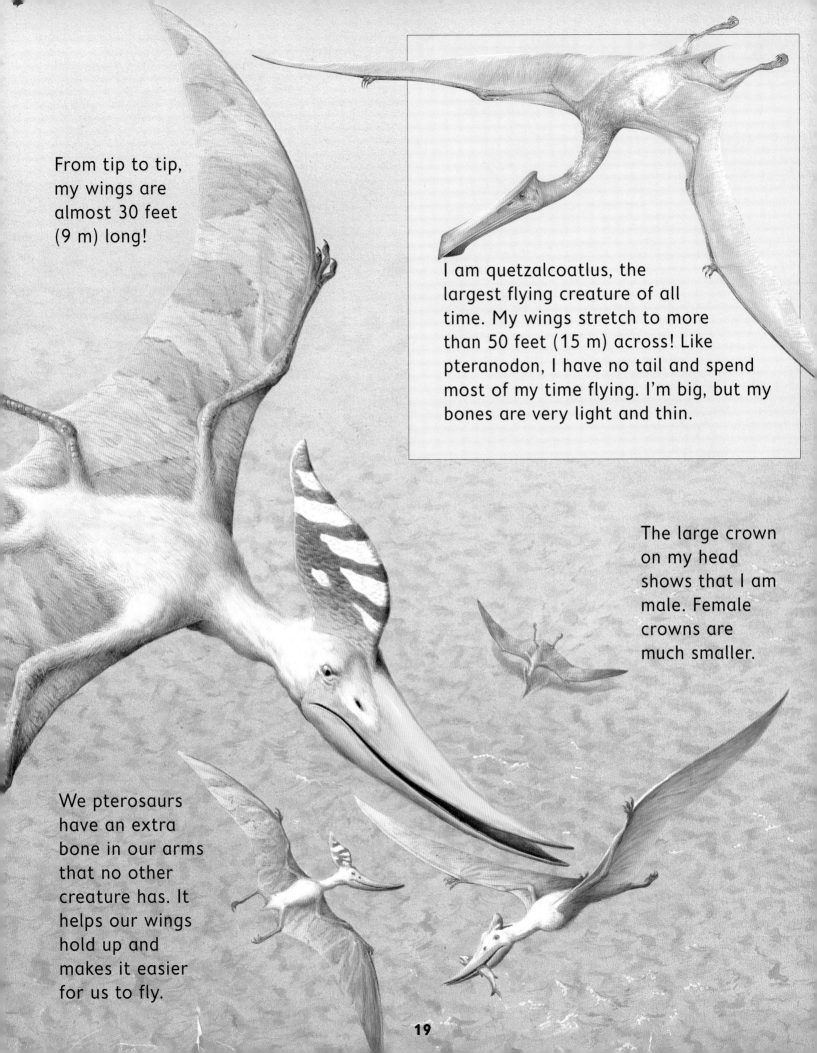

From tip to tip, my wings are almost 30 feet (9 m) long!

I am quetzalcoatlus, the largest flying creature of all time. My wings stretch to more than 50 feet (15 m) across! Like pteranodon, I have no tail and spend most of my time flying. I'm big, but my bones are very light and thin.

The large crown on my head shows that I am male. Female crowns are much smaller.

We pterosaurs have an extra bone in our arms that no other creature has. It helps our wings hold up and makes it easier for us to fly.

Did Reptiles Live Under the Sea?

I am kronosaurus, one of the largest predators in the warm seas of the Jurassic period. I am not a dinosaur but a pliosaur, a giant sea reptile. Like dolphins, I have to come to the surface to breathe.

Ichthyosaurs are also sea reptiles. They prey on fish and shellfish.

My jaws are lined with sharp teeth at the front for catching fish, squid, or ichthyosaurs and dull teeth at the back for crushing the shells of my favorite food, ammonites.

These ammonites are delicious! They are like little squid in a curled-up shell. They often float around in groups, making them easy to catch.

I have a short tail and four large, powerful flippers for swimming. When I swim, I look like I'm flying underwater. My flippers are also useful when I breed. We female pliosaurs have to lay our eggs on beaches. So we pull ourselves onto beaches with our flippers and lay eggs in the sand.

The plesiosaur is related to me, but it has a much longer neck and smaller head. It catches small fish, plankton, squid, and ammonites in the water through rows of long, needlelike teeth, just as some whales do.

How Did a *Tyrannosaurus rex* Hunt?

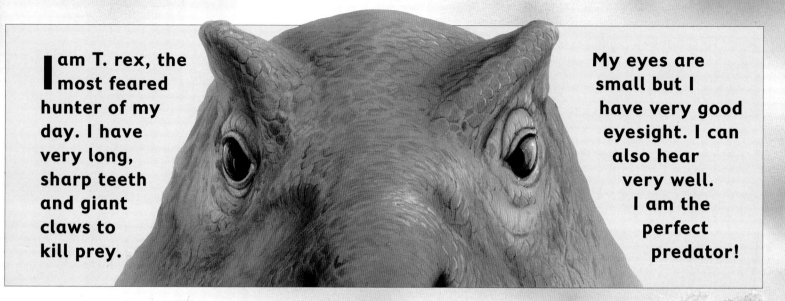

I am T. rex, the most feared hunter of my day. I have very long, sharp teeth and giant claws to kill prey.

My eyes are small but I have very good eyesight. I can also hear very well. I am the perfect predator!

I have a huge nose and a very powerful sense of smell. I can pick up the scent of meat from many miles (km) away. I can't run fast or for very long and I don't want to waste energy chasing my prey. So I often find food by scaring other predators away from their kills.

At the right moment, I jump on this young triceratops. I hold it down with my feet.

My arms are really tiny. But my sharp claws come in handy if I need to pin down my prey.

With my long, knifelike teeth, I killed this dinosaur easily. Few dinosaurs would dare try to steal a meal from under my nose—except maybe another T. rex. We even sometimes eat each other if we have a chance!

Why Did the Dinosaurs Die Out?

The world has changed. When I was a young edmontosaurus, there were plants and water here, and the sky was blue above us. But then one day there was a bright light in the sky, followed by a huge explosion. Since then the sky has been thick with dark clouds.

No plants have grown since the explosion. We have been walking for weeks now looking for more food. But it's the same everywhere. Lots of us have died. Worst of all, it's so cold. Without sun shining through the clouds to warm us, I don't think we can go on much longer.

Birds and these furry animals pick the bones of the dead dinosaurs clean.

There was a streak of light across the sky.

It hit the earth with a huge explosion.

Things were changing even before the bright light. There once was enough food and water, but then the water hole dried up, it rained less, and the world got hotter.

Meat eaters can eat dead dinosaurs. We plant eaters are weak from lack of food and are easy prey for meat eaters. But what will they eat when we've all gone?

Which Bird Hunted Horses?

It is now the Tertiary age and there are no more scary tyrannosaurs or big plant eaters around. But there are lots of warm-blooded furry creatures, called mammals, living here. I am diatryma, also called gastornis. I am the biggest, scariest predator now.

I am a bird, with a bill and feathers, but I'm bigger than any bird you've ever seen. I am taller than the tallest man and weigh as much as a car! I am too big to fly with my small wings, but I do have strong legs so I can run fast enough to catch my prey.

These funny little horses are called hyracotheriums. They are only 1 ½ feet (.5 m) tall and can't run very fast. They live together in herds and eat plants and grass.

I look large and heavy, but my bones are very light. This is how I run so fast.

My large beak is very strong, too. I can crush my prey with a single bite.

Which Animals Lived During the Ice Ages?

These strange, two-legged animals may look small and harmless next to me, but they're very smart. They know how to make fire and use sharpened sticks to hunt animals. Actually, they look a little like you!

We woolly mammoths live in a very cold world now. The ice cap at the North Pole has spread a long way south. The ground is frozen. This is the tundra, where only grasses and short plants can grow in the thin soil. There are no trees.

I am about the size of an elephant, but my thick hair and long, curving tusks make me look bigger. I use my tusks to dig for grass in the snow. Males also use them in fights. I am the herd's leader, the largest and oldest female.

We mammoths live about 70 or 80 years. It will be about 10 years before my son is as big as me. Once the males are grown up, they live on their own, not in herds with females and young.

We use our trunks to pick grass and plants.

We are sabre-toothed cats. We live in South America. It is much warmer here than in the cold northern lands. There is plenty of food around for hungry predators like us to eat. This herd of macrauchenias looks tasty. They are like today's llamas, but they have long trunklike noses.

This rhinoceros is also used to life in the cold. He has two levels of fur: dense, woolly fur underneath and long hair on top. His fur keeps him warm and also stops the rain and snow from getting through to his skin. His horns are made of hard hair, not bone.

We cave bears hibernate through the winter, sleeping in caves. We eat as much as we can during the short summer and autumn to build up fat under our skin. This will keep us warm and nourished throughout our long sleep.

How Did Fossils Form?

My story is a long one. It starts with a terrible event 160 million years ago. I was a mamenchisaurus, a large plant-eating dinosaur. I lived in a large herd. Each year we migrated across the country in search of food . . .

1 One year, we tried to cross a stream in a deep valley. Before we could all cross, a great flood swept through the valley. Those of us still crossing were swept away and drowned. My body was buried in mud. My flesh rotted away until only my bones and teeth were left.

2 Over time, mud and sand from the river slowly piled on top of me, until my bones turned into hard rock.

3 My bones lay buried deep in the rock for millions of years. The river dried up and the land turned to desert. Very slowly, wind and rain wore away the rock on top of me. Some of my bones began to appear on the surface. One day, a boy looking for fossils found me. Scientists carefully dug up my bones. My bones will give them clues about how I lived.

Another type of fossil is held in a sticky sap, called resin, that came from prehistoric trees. The resin oozed out of the tree bark. Unlucky bugs landed in it and got stuck. This fossilized resin is called amber.

This is a fossil of a footprint, made when a dinosaur stepped into some soft mud. The mud hardened and later turned into rock.

Glossary

Cambrian period
(KAM-bree-un PIR-ee-ud) The period of Earth's history about 540–500 million years ago, when advanced life first lived.

Carboniferous period
(kahr-buh-NIH-feh-rus PIR-ee-ud) The period of Earth's history about 355–295 million years ago, when reptiles first appeared.

Cretaceous period
(krih-TAY-shus PIR-ee-ud) The period of Earth's history about 135–65 million years ago, when the largest dinosaurs lived.

Devonian period
(dih-VOH-nee-un PIR-ee-ud) The period of Earth's history about 410–355 million years ago, when land plants, and fish first lived.

Ice ages (YS AYJ-ez) The time in Earth's history when ice sheets spread out from the poles and the Earth was colder.

Jurassic period
(ju-RA-sik PIR-ee-ud) The period of Earth's history 203–135 million years ago, when dinosaurs ruled and the first birds lived.

Migration
(my-GRAY-shun) The movement of animals, to and from where they eat or breed.

Tertiary period
(TER-shee-ur-ee PIR-ee-ud) The period of Earth's history 65–1.75 million years ago, when mammals ruled.

Index

Web Sites

Due to the changing nature of Internet links, PowerKids Press has developed an online list of Web sites related to the subject of this book. This site is updated regularly. Please use this link to access the list: www.powerkidslinks.com/ask/dino/